On Top of Spaghetti

A Song by Tom Glazer ✳ Illustrations by Rob Barber

GoodYearBooks

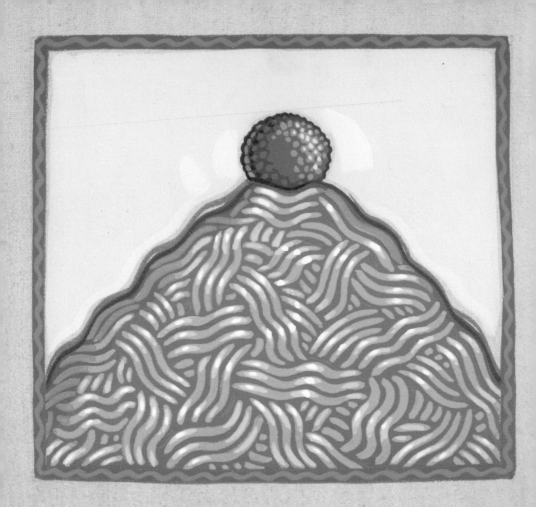

On top of spaghetti,

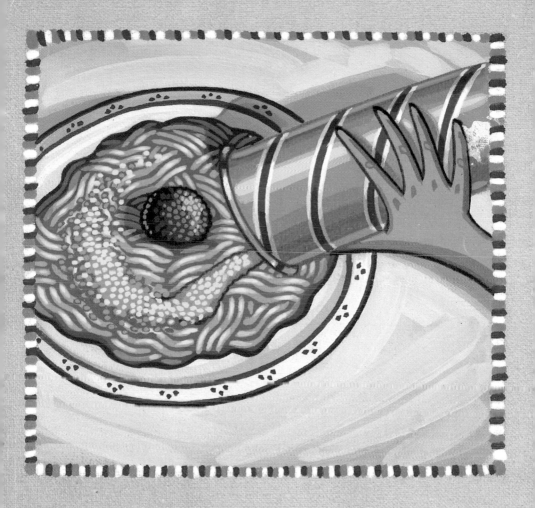

all covered with cheese

I lost my poor meatball

when somebody sneezed.

It rolled off the table
and onto the floor.

And then my poor meatball
rolled out of the door.

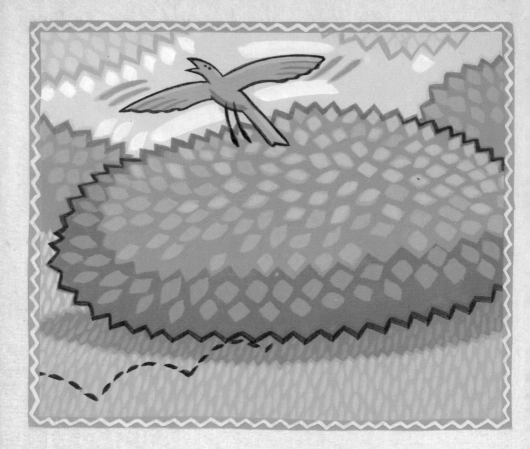

It rolled in the garden
and under a bush.

And then my poor meatball
was nothing but mush.

The mush was as tasty
as tasty could be.

And early next summer
it grew into a tree.

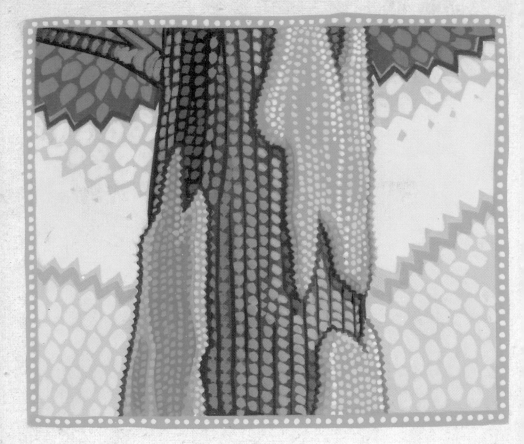

The tree was all covered
with beautiful moss.

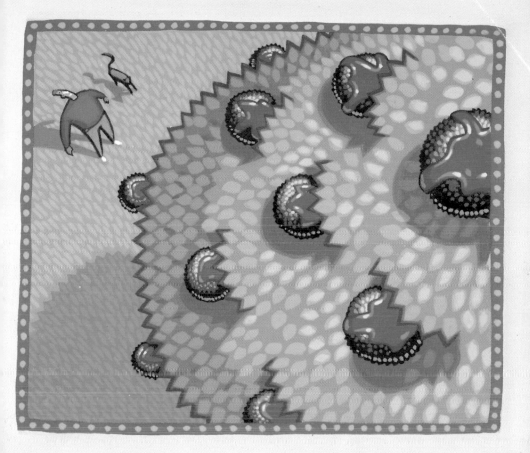

It grew great big meatballs
and tomato sauce.

So if you eat spaghetti

all covered with cheese,

hold on to your meatball
and don't ever sneeze.

16